GREAT SHARKY SHARK

HAPPY READING!

This book is especially for:

_____

Suzanne Tate,
Author—
brings fun and
facts to us in her
Nature Series.

James Melvin,
Illustrator—
brings joyous life
to Suzanne Tate's
characters.

Suzanne and James in costume

GREAT SHARKY SHARK

A Tale of a Big Hunter

Suzanne Tate

Illustrated by James Melvin

Nags Head Art

To Sam Tate

a free spirit — always
on the move!

Library of Congress Catalog Card Number 97-76145
ISBN 978-1-878405-21-0
ISBN 1-878405-21-7
Published by
Nags Head Art, Inc., P.O. Box 2149, Manteo, NC 27954
Copyright © 1998 by Suzanne Tate
Revised 2005

Great Sharky Shark was young and bold.
He was a big hunter from the day he was born.

He was tough and rough — a White Shark!
Thousands of tiny teeth-like points
covered his body.

Great Sharky Shark went looking for food all the time.
His sense of smell was superb.

He could tell from a tiny, tiny smell
if there was something to eat nearby.

And he was always on the move.
If he didn't keep moving,
he would simply sink!

Great Sharky Shark liked to hunt alone for food.
He always stayed clear of bigger sharks
that might eat him!

But he didn't mind when his sister swam nearby.
She was a little smaller than he.

One day, the two young sharks swam
near an old SHIPWRECK.
"This is where I am going to hunt for food,"
Great Sharky said.
"That's a good idea," his sister said.
"I will hunt here too."

Great Sharky and his sister swam
in and around the old wreck.
They could easily turn and twist
because there were no true bones in their bodies.

There was plenty of food at the SHIPWRECK.
Great Sharky Shark ate so fast that some of his teeth fell out!
But he didn't worry about it!
He knew that new teeth would move
forward in his jaw right away.

Great Sharky Shark and his sister scared away all
the fish around the SHIPWRECK.
"Where did they go?" he asked.
"Silly!" his sister said. "If you were a little fish,
would you stay here with us?"

"Well, I'm still hungry," replied Great Sharky Shark.
"I'd like to be a great big White Shark.
Then I could catch seals and sea lions."

"Maybe I'll go somewhere else to hunt," Great Sharky said.
"I can find lots of fish at the TRASH PLACE."
"That's not a good idea," his sister said sternly.
"HUMANS always leave a lot of junk there.
If you eat junk, it might make you sick."

"We sharks hardly ever get sick no matter what we eat," Great Sharky said.
"Remember that shark we heard about that ate a tin can, shoes and a life jacket?"

"But that was a Tiger Shark," his sister replied.
"They eat anything, even other sharks."

Great Sharky Shark wouldn't listen to his sister.
He swam away fast by moving
his tail briskly.

Soon Great Sharky came to the TRASH PLACE.
Fish swirled all around him.
He chased a little fish through a tower of trash.

When he came out on the other side,
Great Sharky had a plastic ring around his head!

He turned and twisted, but that ring had stuck fast.
Great Sharky Shark was unhappy!
He swam quickly away from the TRASH PLACE.

His sister was surprised the next time she saw him.
"What happened to you?" she asked.
"I can't get this ring off my head," he sighed.
"It was at the TRASH PLACE."

"Now you see that I was right," his sister said. "The TRASH PLACE is no good for anybody. I don't know why HUMANS throw things in the water."

"Well, maybe I'll get this ring off soon," Great Sharky said, trying to be happy.

But days went by and weeks went by.
And that ring — like a big collar —
was still on Great Sharky's head.

Little shells and barnacles began to grow on it.
And every day, the ring grew a little heavier.

One day, Great Sharky Shark was swimming near
the SHIPWRECK again.
He found lots of fish to eat.

He didn't notice the shadow of a big shark —
a great big Tiger Shark!

Great Sharky swam through an opening in the SHIPWRECK.
Suddenly, his shell collar was caught
on a jagged piece of wood!

And that great big Tiger Shark swam closer and closer.

Great Sharky Shark was scared when he saw
that big stranger with his mouthful of sharp teeth.

"I'm the one being hunted now," he thought.
"I'll turn and twist and try to get loose."

Just in time, his shell collar pulled off on the
jagged timber and went spinning through the water.
It landed on one of the great big Tiger Shark's teeth!
Great Sharky Shark turned tail fast!

He was hunting in safer waters
when he saw his sister.
"I'm sure you are happy to be free
of that heavy collar," she said.

"Yes," Great Sharky Shark replied. "I hope I don't ever again run into trash left by HUMANS."

"Let's hope HELPFUL HUMANS will work to keep the water clean," his sister said.
"Then it will be a nicer world for all of us."